JASMINE'S
JOURNEY

JASMINE'S JOURNEY

(I Know I Been Changed)

WRITTEN BY

LIVINGSTON HOLLOWAY

ILLUSTRATED BY

LINK LACAILLE

JASMINE'S JOURNEY
(I KNOW I BEEN CHANGED)

iUniverse books may be ordered through booksellers or by contacting:

iUniverse
1663 Liberty Drive
Bloomington, IN 47403
www.iuniverse.com
1-800-Authors (1-800-288-4677)

ISBN: 978-1-4917-6266-0 (sc)
ISBN: 978-1-4917-6267-7 (hc)
ISBN: 978-1-4917-6268-4 (e)

Library of Congress Control Number: 2015903883

Print information available on the last page.

iUniverse rev. date: 3/9/2015

CONTENTS

Dedication

To Dr. Adelaide L. Sanford

Former principal of the Crispus Attucks
School (PS 21) in Brooklyn, New York

Former vice chancellor of the NewYork
State Board of Regents

Be as a bird perched on a frail branch
that she feels beneath her,
Still she sings away—all the same—
knowing that she has wings.
—Victor Hugo

ACKNOWLEDGMENTS

Thanks to Mars Alma and the iUniverse staff for its professional attention to the compiling of this book. Also a special thanks to Pamela Holloway, Cecelia Johnson, Takada Walls, Nzingha Abena (Queen Mother), Erica Blake, Tony Williams aka Professor Tony, Dorothy Williams, Link Lacille and the entire Lacille family, Germaul Barnes, Germaine Behagen, Phyllis Smith, Kimberly Johnson, Betty Vandegrift-Greene, Indigo Gill, Songhay Parham, Hortensia Gooding, Zahir, Lydia, and Dr. Felicia El-Amin.

DC Woodson Middle School

CHAPTER 1
At DC Woodson Middle School

I hate it here. It's boring here. I don't want to be here. I have to get out of here. It's boring here. I don't want to be here!

Jasmine wrote on her desk.

I wrote that on my desk, top to bottom, in the classroom. Then I took out my blue highlighter and drew pictures of hearts in my class notebook. As I drew, I thought about my dad. My dad was in the US Army. I missed him. I stopped drawing. I sat still and thought a little more: *Some folks think that troublemakers are annoying people who just want attention. And you know what? A lot of them are. But I am not a troublemaker. It's just that it's boring here. I don't like it here. I have to get out of here.*

"So, class, this week will be an eventful week! We are going to spend some quality time with an African American historian," Mrs. Truth said.

"What is an African American historian?" Zahir asked.

Mrs. Truth's eyes expanded, and she quickly glanced at all the scholars' faces to see if the whole class was curious. "That's a great question!" said Mrs. Truth. "An African American historian is a person who has studied African history and culture and one who speaks the truth."

"Wow!" the class responded joyfully.

I whispered to myself but loud enough for others to hear, "Who cares?"

I hate it here. I hate it here. I don't want to be here. It is so boring here. I don't understand why anyone would want to be in this school. Basically, at this point in my life, the only thing that matters to me is my dad. I hate it here. I hate it here. I don't want to be here. I have to get out of here.

I wrote on my desk again. This desk was going to tell plenty of folks about me. They'd see that I could be a mean kid. I was not bad looking, but I was just so mean and angry that no one ever really wanted to be around me. Plus, sometimes I just liked to yell at people and call them bad names. Most of the skirts I wore were too large for my small body. I was really small for my age. Anyway, that didn't matter since I was not bad looking, and I had much longer hair than most of the girls in this class. *Okay,* I thought, *I'll start drawing more pictures on this desk. Hmmm …I'll draw a picture of me yelling at the teachers. And I'll draw a picture of me throwing my textbooks in the trash bin.*

"This is a big deal!" said Mrs. Truth. Then she looked sternly at me and asked, "Jasmine, what makes you think this is no big deal?"

"I already know about African history …and I also know we were slaves and we were sold on auction blocks. No more auction blocks for me, no more, no more. No more auction blocks for me—many thousand gone. I got to get to freedom, got to get to Freedom Land. I want out of here. I don't want to be here. I will get out of here."

Mrs. Truth gasped as my words reached her ears, and she walked over to me and said carefully, "Well, Jasmine, slavery is only a small part of our history."

"Oh, please, Mrs. Truth. What's the point? In the end, people only think of us as slaves. We are descendants of African slaves. No more auction blocks for me. No more!" I yelled out as tears rolled down my cheeks and onto my desk.

"Oh, my dear Jasmine, I am sure you will change your tune once you meet this great historian," said Mrs. Truth.

I hate it here. It is boring here. I don't want to be here. I really need to get out of here. I hate it here. It's boring here!

I'd been thinking, though, that I could sit here and continue to draw pictures on this desk. Like I said, this desk was going to tell a whole story about me. I drew pictures of me hanging out in the school yard. Everyone seemed to have someone to play with, but not me. I preferred hanging out by myself. I promised myself never to go out at lunchtime from now on. I was not going to pretend to be friends with my classmates. Besides, who would want to be friends with me? All of my classmates were cooperating with Mrs. Truth because they wanted to get good grades. They all wanted to go to high school. As for me, I really got annoyed by some of the dumb questions they asked her. Everybody thought I was rude. They didn't understand me. I really didn't like being here. It was so boring here.

The only one who really knew me and knew how I felt about anything was my awesome dad. I really needed to work on getting out of DC Woodson Middle School. I was tired of being in this school. I was tired of learning about things that didn't interest me. *No more auction blocks for me—many thousand gone. Got to get to freedom! Got to get to Freedom Land!*

"Got to get to Freedom Land!"

CHAPTER 2
The Next Day

"Good morning, scholars! This morning we will spend a major part of our classroom time with our African American historian," said Mrs. Truth.

"What does he plan to do with us?"

"That's a great question, Jasmine!" said Mrs. Truth. "Our African American historian plans on engaging all of us in some interesting activities related to our African history and culture. He has also planned an interesting trip for us to visit the Smithsonian Institution."

I just don't understand the point of all this, I thought. *I will give this learning activity a try—I just might like it. Life is different for me, always has been since Dad's been gone. So this is no big deal. So here's the final deal: this learning experience better be about something!*

"Okay, scholars, I believe Garvey, our African American historian, has arrived," Mrs. Truth said. She pointed toward the classroom door and grabbed the students' attention.

Mrs. Truth introduced historian Garvey to her scholars.

"Good morning!" Garvey said. "I need all of you to repeat after me. Say *amee.*"

"Amee!" the scholars shouted with great excitement in their voices.

"Amee means you are paying attention. *Ago*," shouted Garvey. "Ago means may I have your attention?"

"Amee!" said the scholars.

Wow, I wasn't writing on my desk at this moment. I was also surprised to notice that this so-called historian looked much younger than me. Hmmm ...about ten years of age. Garvey was extremely short, and he was wearing dress pants and a solid-colored shirt. He looked like one of those little men who worked in a checking and savings bank. Garvey's fluffy hairstyle made him look quite unique. He really didn't look like he knew anything about African history and culture. But, then again, maybe he did. This just didn't make sense, and it wasn't realistic that someone much younger than me would know more than I did. *Maybe he's a genius? Hmm ...I might give Garvey a chance to prove that he is a historian.*

"Okay, scholars," said Garvey. "Please join me as we embark on a wonderful journey of learning about some aspects of our African history and culture."

"Awesome!"

Mrs. Truth said, "Please continue, Garvey."

"Why, of course," he said and recited:

"We are a people of color.

We are from ancient Nubia to Egyptian mysteries.

We are black, bold, and beautiful.
Civilizations of kings and queens,
King Tut and Queen Nefertari,
Rulers of the world.
We lived in palaces.
We built the great pyramids."

"Isn't that part of the Nubian pledge you recited?" asked Mrs. Truth.

"Yes!" said Garvey.

My dad had been gone for three years. I couldn't stop thinking about him. And every day, when I walked into this school, I thought about him. "Jasmine, you are going to do your very best in school," my dad would say. He would always tell me to be nice to people. "Jasmine, try to find the good in people, whatever situation you find yourself in." Of course, once Dad left I didn't think about the good, but I knew that if he were here, he would remind me to be good. But just knowing that he was not, oh well ...Anyway, I would enter DC Woodson and my classroom, and I would work real hard. My dad was so proud of me. *Well, Jasmine,* I said to myself, *try not to turn it up in this here classroom. Ha-ha!*

"Mrs. Truth," I called out. The words just seemed to pop out of my mouth. "How can this little man be an authority on African history?"

"I tell you what," said Mrs. Truth, "we will have our 'little man' tell us a little about himself."

"Very funny, Mrs. Truth!" I said out loud so the whole class could hear and laugh.

"Please, Jasmine, I will not tolerate you calling out in this classroom," Mrs. Truth said. "I will also give all of you scholars an opportunity to ask Garvey questions in regard to how he became an historian."

"Greetings again to you, my dear scholars. As you know, my name is Garvey. I am a ten-year-old African American. My favorite subjects are African history, global history, and math. I began learning about various aspects of African history and culture at the Uhur School, which is an independent private school located in Baltimore, Maryland. The more knowledge I gained about African history, the more I wanted to share what I learned with others. My teachers were so excited about my ability to retain all the information that I learned about Africa."

Jasmine stood up from her desk and asked, "How did you get so passionate about African history and culture?"

"That's a great question," Garvey said. "African history is so cool. I like the fact that all humanity began in Africa."

"Garvey, you are no real historian," I said.

"Sit down, Jasmine; please sit down!" said Mrs. Truth

"But I have more to say."

"I repeat, Jasmine, please sit down!" Mrs. Truth said.

"This is ridiculous, Mrs. Truth. Garvey is not a historian."

I went to the front of the class and started singing, "No more auction blocks for me." I rocked back and forth till I hit my head on the Smart Board. I started stomping my feet on the floor and shouting, "I'm turning it up in here."

Garvey looked at me. "Jasmine, are you all right?"

"Yes," I said. "Are you all right? You're make-believe—"

"Okay, scholars, let's get back on the subject," said Garvey.

"No!" I shouted. I start walking over to Mrs. Truth, knocking on every desk I passed. I pushed him. "Tell me, Garvey, seriously, how a little boy of ten years old can be an expert on African history. You're a fake!"

"Sit down, Jasmine!" Mrs. Truth said.

"Okay!" I answered as I went back to my seat.

When I was seated, Mrs. Truth told Garvey that he could continue with his presentation.

"Also, my dear scholars, always remember," he said, "that we come from a great people:

We come from a great people;

We must be great too.

We come from a mighty people;

We must be mighty too.

We come from a caring people;

We must be caring too.

We come from a giving people;

We must be giving too.

We come from a thinking people;

We must be thinkers too.

We come from an intelligent people;

We must be intelligent too.

We come from a great people;

We must be great too."

"Master Garvey, I recently heard that you are planning to write some books on African history and culture," said Mrs. Truth.

"Why yes," said Garvey. "I am in the process of researching the life of Dr. John Henrik Clarke, a public intellectual and a great African American historian. I am really interested in writing a book about this awesome man."

It had been two hours since Garvey had arrived, and things were just like always, only I was trying to cooperate and listen to him. I mean, I did not write on my desk. And I really enjoyed listening to this so-called historian. I was trying to hold on, to do the right thing, but I kept having memories of my dad, about how much I missed him. And I felt like doing my classwork was not worth all the effort. *Why should I behave in school, follow instructions, and listen to my teachers?* I thought.

One time my dad found out I had been bad in school. I told him I disrespected the teacher. I yelled at her. Oh yes, I did. Ha-ha! Then I jumped up, ran to the front of the classroom, and pounded my fist against the chalkboard. Then I ran out of the classroom. Yes I did. Ha-ha! I did not like that teacher. My dad did not say anything though. He just said I better never, ever yell or be disrespectful to Mrs. Jones again. Wow, that was three years ago. It was the beginning of sixth grade. That was the last year my dad was home.

"What's next?" I asked Mrs. Truth.

"It's time for lunch!" she said. "Scholars, during lunch please make sure you share some of the historical facts you learned about Africa with the scholars from the other eighth grade classes."

"Yes, Mrs. Truth!" said the students.

"Okay, scholars, we need to hurry to the lunchroom," Mrs. Truth said as they walked toward the classroom door.

I really hated lunchtime! I had my reasons. I didn't like most of the food in that lunchroom. There was, however, one great cook. The scholars called her Aunt Cookie. Yes, I liked Aunt Cookie because she made the best chocolate cookies in DC. She also made delicious chocolate cupcakes. Mmm … tasty and extremely good. When we went to lunch, most of the scholars played outside in the school yard. I, however, chose to participate in the "Lunch and Learn" sessions.

CHAPTER 3
Lunch and Learn

DC Woodson Middle School was huge, and lots of kids went to this school. Although the building was large, it was only two stories high. There was a big school yard where the scholars played. The yard had handball courts, basketball courts, and lot of benches to sit on. Almost all the boys played basketball or handball. The girls mostly jumped rope. Some of the girls just sat on the benches and talked about stupid stuff like their favorite television show or the music they liked to listen to.

Lunch consisted of dry hamburgers and french fries. When I was finished eating, I headed for the Lunch and Learn Resource Room. It was about 12:15 p.m. I wondered, *Is today's activity going to be interesting? Is it going to be fun?* I made myself behave even though I wanted to cause trouble and chaos. Ha-ha! People didn't notice me all that much unless I did something wrong. Oh, I could wreak some havoc during lunchtime. I, however, went to my Lunch and Learn desk and sat quietly in my seat. This time I wouldn't give myself a chance to turn it up or fool around. I immediately started listening to Ms. Nzingha, the Lunch and Learn instructor. Ms. Nzingha was mad-cool. She was always smiling. She always looked happy. Ms. Nzingha had dark brown hair, and she was small in stature. I really liked her. She didn't bother me like some of my other teachers.

"Good afternoon, scholars!" said Ms. Nzingha. "Take a good look at the quotations on the Smart Board. Read each one very carefully."

"Nothing is more powerful and liberating than knowledge."
William H. Grey III, US Congressman
"Knowledge is power, and power is
the key to changing things."
Jill Nelson, author and journalist
"The most beautiful thing about learning is
that no one can take it away from you."
B. B. King, musician
"College is for everyone!"
Queen Nzingha Abena, retired New York City educator

"Today, you will spend the rest of your lunchtime creating bookmarks," Ms. Nzingha said. "Think about the mood you were in when you read the quotations. Pick one quotation that inspired you the most. Write the quotation on your bookmark. Think about artwork you can add to your bookmark to express the mood the quotation evoked in you.

"Jasmine, I didn't know if you would be participating in today's Lunch and Learn activity," Ms. Nzingha said as she stuffed some leftover fries into her mouth. "I am so glad you decided to cooperate."

"Sorry for yesterday!" I said apologetically.

Ms. Nzingha shook her head. "You don't have anything to apologize for Jasmine. I am just glad you are here and working."

I sat up. "Look, Ms. Nzingha, I am capable of sitting up in my seat and doing my classwork. I am trying to get it together. I am trying to do more work during the school hours."

Ms. Nzingha nodded. *But not quickly enough*, I thought. "Jasmine, it will be a long time before you are actually able to complete your incomplete assignments. We need to come up with a plan or strategy for you to complete prior Lunch and Learn assignments."

"The only way for that to happen is …maybe I can stay after school to complete my assignments," I said with much concern.

"No problem, Jasmine," said Ms. Nzingha. "I will speak to your teacher, Mrs. Truth, to see if that's possible."

Then Ms. Nzingha tapped on her desk with her pencil while the scholars were working on making their bookmarks. "Would any scholars care to share their thoughts or reflections on today's activity?"

"Yes, Ms. Nzingha!" I said, standing up from my seat to answer the question. "Knowledge is power!"

"Jasmine, that's an interesting reflection," the teacher said.

It was one o'clock in the afternoon when we finished making the bookmarks. I really did not want to go. I wanted to stay there a little longer, but I followed the instructions given to me from Ms. Nzingha. On the way to class, I kept wondering when my dad would return home. Every day after school my dad would buy me chocolate cupcakes or chocolate ice cream for an after-school treat. And dad would ask me questions about what I had learned in school. I sure missed him. I remembered the time me and Dad went roller skating. It was the most fun thing we did together. "Don't fall, Jasmine!" my dad would shout as we skated around the rink near DC Middle School.

CHAPTER 4

Inside Mrs. Truth's Transformed Classroom

As the scholars returned from Lunch and Learn, they were amazed at the transformation of their classroom. Inside the room were eight new tables—four circles and four rectangles. There was a large rug in one corner with a picture of Africa woven in bright colors. There was also a classroom library filled with a collection of African history books, a map of the world, an Arts and Crafts Learning Center, and in the corner Mrs. Truth's new desk.

"Okay, scholars, please sit at any table of your choice," Mrs. Truth said.

"Mrs. Truth," I called out.

"Yes, Jasmine," she said.

"Where should I sit?" I asked.

"Jasmine, there appears to be some available seats at the rectangular table where Lydia and Zahir are seated. Please do yourself a favor and sit there!" Mrs. Truth said firmly.

"Also, Mrs. Truth," I said, "I volunteer to be group leader. And I think Lydia should be the secretary."

"No fair!" Lydia yelled. "I want to be with my friends!"

"Settle down, Lydia. It's time to begin today's lesson," said Mrs. Truth.

"That's right, Lydia, settle down!" I said.

"Jasmine, please do not volunteer your classmates without their approval," Mrs. Truth said sternly.

"Scholars," she continued, "this afternoon's assignment is as follows: You will read an article called 'The Early Life of King Tut.' After reading the article, you will share your thoughts and reactions with your team members who are seated at your table. Each table shall have one group leader to facilitate discussion and one secretary to record notes. Does everyone understand?"

"Yes!" said the scholars.

After reading the text, I asked my classmate Zahir to share his thoughts or reaction to the article. Zahir laughed and said, "Jasmine, we haven't decided that you are the group leader."

"No more auction blocks for me. I *am* the group leader," I said. "Now, Zahir, please share your reaction to the article."

"Okay, Jasmine, my favorite part was when I found out that King Tut was one of the best-known pharaohs of ancient Egypt."

"That's great information, Zahir. What else did you learn?"

"I also found out that in 1922 archaeologists discovered King Tut's intact tomb."

"Indeed they did, Zahir," I said. "And that led many to unravel the mysteries of King Tut's life and death."

"What about me, Jasmine?" Lydia shouted.

"Go ahead and speak, Lydia."

"Well, Jasmine, I found out that King Tut was born in 1341 BCE and that he was the twelfth king of the eighteenth Egyptian dynasty."

"Great job, Lydia!" I said. "I really like the fact that King Tut's remains have led millions to be in awe over the mystery of his life and death."

"Okay, scholars, now that everyone has shared with each other in their respective groups, let us move on and read some more articles and books about famous Africans," Mrs. Truth said.

"No thanks," I murmured. "I will not read any more articles. I am about ready to turn it up in here. I enjoyed reading and learning about King Tut, but that was enough for me!"

King Tut's intact tomb

"Jasmine, there has got to be some more information about Africa that you want to learn," Zahir said.

"Mind your own business, Zahir!" I said angrily. "That's enough for me! The television shows and movies have taught me all I need to know about African history."

"Now, now, Jasmine, I want you to calm yourself down and show Master Garvey that you appreciate his visit," Mrs. Truth said.

I stood up from my desk and walked out. That's right, I walked out. And as I walked out of that classroom, I overheard:

"Mrs. Truth, did I say something to Jasmine that offended her, or is she upset because I brought so many articles and books for the scholars to read?" asked Garvey.

"I don't think so," Mrs. Truth said. "Jasmine always walks out of the classroom."

Garvey followed me out into the hallway. He crossed his arms and leaned against the wall. "Jasmine, listen up."

I looked into his piercing eyes. "No more, Garvey!" I said as big tears rolled down my cheeks onto the floor.

"Jasmine," Garvey said, "did you know that Africa is a continent and that there are fifty-two countries in Africa?"

I shook my head and cried out, "No, Garvey, I didn't know! Please leave me alone."

"And Jasmine, Africa has more gold, jewels, copper, and platinum than any other continent."

"Wow, Garvey, you can't be serious," I said.

"Yes, Jasmine, I am definitely serious," said Garvey. "Did you know that

- the Nile River is the longest river in the world;
- scientists tell us that the first men and women on earth lived in Africa more than four million years ago;
- archaeologists have uncovered the oldest human skeletons in Tanzania; and
- the first civilizations and the first cities were found in Africa?"

I shook my head. "Garvey, I didn't know that we come from such a great people. Please tell me more."

"Okay, Jasmine," Garvey said. "Did you know that the people of Kemit (ancient Egypt) called their language Medu-Neter? Medu-Neter was written and spoken by African people for over five thousand years. Two components of the language are sound and picture signs. Medu-Neter is written from left to right."

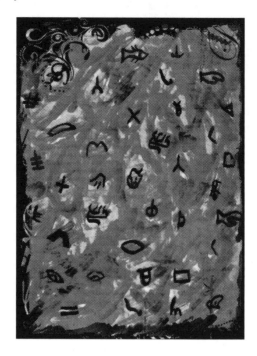

My eyes stared wide as I shook my head with excitement and said, "No more auction blocks for me. Garvey, please tell me more."

"Why certainly, Jasmine!" said Garvey. "Did you know that most pyramids were made of limestone and granite? Also the pyramids were built during the reigns of native African kings and queens. The Great Pyramid of Knufu is considered one of the seven wonders of the ancient world. The Knufu pyramid was built using 2,300,000 blocks of stone weighing two and a half tons each."

The Great Pyramid

"Wow, this is awesome information!"

"Yes, Jasmine. I hope that what I have shared with you has given you some desire to gain more knowledge about Africa," said Garvey. "Now let's get back into the classroom."

"Okay!" I said.

"Jasmine, whenever I do good things, I feel like I'm representing my family in a positive way. It's great knowing that when I do well, I'm making sure my family will be proud of me," he said.

"Garvey, that's exactly how I felt when my dad was home. I would feel great about my accomplishments in my classwork. I am so glad we are so much alike."

"Yes, doing good things is how we honor ourselves and our family. Now let's get back to work," he said.

"Exactly!" I replied.

Upon entering the classroom, I went to my seat and began writing in my journal notebook.

May 2014
Dear Journal:

I am a firm believer in the benefits of attending school and receiving a solid education. However, after missing my dad, I am concerned that I have a negative attitude in regard to school and obtaining an education.

I say that I don't want to read, and sometimes I don't feel the need to gain further knowledge on various topics. I think I need to realize that my education is the key to me having a successful future.

I often say that I do not like school. What are my plans for the future? What do I want to be when I become an adult? Does anything good in life come easy? It takes hard work and a willingness to learn and most of all to remember what I have learned.

At times saying, "I had enough or I am tired of this or that ..." is simply an excuse for being lazy. I must discipline myself to do the thing I think I cannot do.

The most important habit I must develop in my life is to read. To gain a good job for the future, it is imperative that I continue to read and learn more. To have a good future, I must change my attitude about school.

Please also note that I feel it is important for me to learn more about Africa. As stated by Dr. Arthur Lewin in his book *Africa is Not a Country: It's a Continent*, "You know about the countries of Europe and the states of the United States. But how much do you know about the fifty-two countries in Africa?" What else do I know about Africa besides the slavery aspects? It is hard to be proud of a place that I do not know, especially when everything I used to hear about Africa was negative. I will not have a real future until I know about my past.

As Garvey stated, "I come from a great people; I must be great too!"

Sincerely,

Jasmine

8th grade student

DC Woodson Middle School

(Write about upcoming trip.)

CHAPTER 5

Day Three: The National Museum of African Art

It was a long ride from DC Woodson Middle School to the National Museum of African Art at the Smithsonian Institution. Unfortunately, some of the scholars did not eat before getting on the hot school bus, so we had to stop three times for them to get breakfast. It seemed like we would never get to our destination. Finally, we turned down a green, grassy road, and as we got closer, I could see the Smithsonian Institution. Wow, I'd never been to a place like this. There were people everywhere, sitting outside on benches or sitting in parked buses and vans. Children were everywhere too. The Museum of African Art is located in a large garden near the Smithsonian Castle. The museum is a large building with only one step to climb before reaching the entrance—and there appeared to be lots of kids getting ready to go inside.

"Yes," I said, "I think this is going to be a terrific trip!"

As the bus got closer to the museum, I could see Garvey coming out of the main entrance to meet us.

"Everyone out!" said our bus driver as he turned off the engine and opened the door to let us scholars out.

"Welcome to the Smithsonian's African Art Museum," Garvey said. "I will be your first tour guide for today. Here at this museum, there is something wonderful, interesting, and amazing to see in every section of the building, and I chose this specific site as it includes several exhibits that focus on African history and culture."

"I am so excited. I am glad I decided to attend this trip!" I murmured.

"Jasmine, I am glad that you and all your classmates are in attendance," Garvey said. "Today, we will also attend an African Studies Workshop."

"That's awesome," I said.

Garvey continued speaking. "Keep in mind that part of the mission of the Smithsonian Institution in regard to African art is to inspire conversation about the beauty, power, and diversity of African arts and cultures worldwide."

"Now let us make our way into the African Arts lecture room," said Mrs. Truth. "I believe they are ready to start in a few minutes."

The African Arts lecture room was very large with rows and rows of chairs. The chairs were old and painted dark brown. If you sat too fast, you would hit your back on the back of the chair, and it would hurt.

"Ouch!" I shouted.

Hanging in the lecture room was a single portrait of Mrs. Mary McLeod Bethune.

"Woo-hoo! Woo-hoo!" I shouted at the top of my lungs as I pointed to the portrait on the wall. "That is a wonderful picture of Mrs. Bethune."

"Yes it is, Jasmine, but will you please lower your voice?" Mrs. Truth whispered in my ear.

"Wow, Mrs. Truth, I'm actually standing next to a portrait of a famous African American."

"Yes, Jasmine," Mrs. Truth continued, "I'm glad you're excited, but—"

"I know, but I must use my quiet voice."

"Exactly!" Mrs. Truth said as she gave me a gentle hug.

It isn't right that Dad is not here, I thought. *It's been a long time since he left me.* I sometimes thought that he might never return home. So why was I excited about this trip? Well, guess what …Mrs. Truth wants me to be quiet …so I won't have anything to say from this point on. I'm going to be still and quiet for a long while. I am going to find me a seat and sit down. Sometimes I really don't like attending these class trips, as I start daydreaming and thinking about my dad.

Mary McLeod Bethune

"Scholars," said Garvey, "I believe the lecture and presentation are about to begin."

"Good morning, DC Woodson Middle School scholars. Welcome to the National Museum of African Art at the Smithsonian Institution. My name is Professor Olatunde, and I will be your lecturer for this morning's presentation.

"Ago," he said.

"Amee!" said the scholars.

Professor Olatunde continued, "Today you will have an opportunity to watch me create a gara cloth. Gara products are a symbol of national identity in Sierra Leone. It's believed that gara dyeing was brought to Sierra Leone between 1840 and 1900 by Mandingo traders from nearby Guinea. In the past, chiefs and warriors used traditionally woven cloth dyed with gara for ceremonial dress, bridal dowry, burial cloths, and gifts for important visitors. Today the word *gara* is used to describe the dyeing process and products, which are now worn by a much wider circle of people."

"Yes!" Lydia said. "This is such a great trip!"

"I'm glad you're enjoying it," said Garvey.

After Professor Olatunde's presentation, we were invited to create our own gara cloth. After making the cloth, we were told it was time to leave for our trip back to school.

It was another long ride from the Smithsonian Institution to DC Woodson Middle School. As we were riding, we passed by the Washington, DC, Mall. The mall is a wonderful place, especially at night when the theaters are jammed with people going to see the latest movies and buying all the freshly popped popcorn that smells so delicious.

Once we got off the bus, it took us only a minute to get back inside the school.

"Hurry, scholars," said Mrs. Truth. "I'd like to give you tonight's homework and send all of you home."

I sighed and went into the classroom. All the scholars followed me. Mrs. Truth handed out the homework packets and walked us to the school's exit doors. Then I started down the street. I was on my way to Grandma's house. As I walked I started to think about Africa and also about my dad.

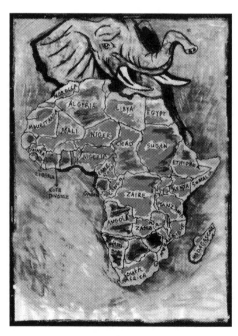

Africa

CHAPTER 6
At Grandma's House

Before I got to Grandma's house, my classmate Zahir stopped me.

"Hey, Jasmine, I'd like you to meet my new neighbor, Omo. Omo plans on attending DC Woodson Middle School."

"Really, Zahir?" I said and continued walking and talking. "Well, hello, Omo. Nice to meet you."

"Nice meeting you also, Jasmine!" Omo said enthusiastically. "I'll be attending DC Woodson tomorrow, and hopefully I will be in the same class as you and Zahir."

"Whatever!" I answered back.

Omo looked grown up. He was very tall, and he looked like a professional basketball player.

"Where are you going, Jasmine? Your house is the other way." Zahir pointed.

"Listen, Zahir," I said, "mind your own business."

I sighed and decided to turn down Tindley Street. It's mostly an all-dirt road. Most people didn't walk down Tindley Street, but I did. I could see Grandma's house in the distance.

Zahir and Omo waved good-bye to me. I waved back and said, "See you guys. I got to hurry to Grandma's house."

Oops, I didn't want Zahir in my business. Oh well! I whispered to myself.

When I finally got to Grandma's house, she came to the door and unlocked the iron gate. Grandma hugged me real tight. Then she gave me this: "How come you took so long to get here?" I just ignored her and walked into her house.

The inside of Grandma's house was nice and clean. Her home was always very warm and comfortable. As I entered her living room, I noticed her beautiful, large mahogany bookshelves. On the shelves were rows and rows of books written by African American authors, a collection of seashells, and several small paintings depicting famous African Americans, such as Martin Luther King Jr., Malcolm X, Marcus Garvey, Rosa Parks, Fannie Lou Hamer, Shirley Chisholm, and, of course, my favorite, Mary McLeod Bethune. I was also astounded by the giant flowered quilt hanging on one of the walls in Grandma's living room.

"No television," she whispered. "How are you going to complete your homework? And no snack! You must concentrate. You must be serious. You need to graduate. Jasmine, you must go to high school."

"Yes, Grandma!"

Now homework was always easy for me since I liked to read. That happened to me because I got bored so easily, and I really didn't have and had never had any real friends. Well, I did have some imaginary friends when I was about six years old. I used to play imaginary school all the time, and of course I had imaginary friends who I played with at lunchtime. I was really supersmart, but I just stopped working so hard because my dad left.

"You haven't finished your homework?" Grandma asked. "Jasmine, are you feeling all right?"

I looked into my grandmother's eyes. I didn't want her to worry about me. "Grandma, I'm okay. I don't feel sick," I said. "I'm just thinking about my dad."

Grandma tilted her head quickly. "Jasmine, hurry up and finish your homework!"

"I will finish it soon!" I said.

After I was done with my homework, Grandma gave me a great big hug and sent me into the kitchen for my usual snack of chocolate cupcakes and chocolate milk.

Grandma walked into the kitchen and gave me another hug. "Jasmine, what color is freedom?" she asked.

"Black!" I said.

"I think if freedom were a color, it would be red." Grandma turned on the heat under her teapot and put a cup on her kitchen table. She poured hot water into her cup and dipped her teabag into the cup as she sat down. "Or maybe it would be yellow like the daises that bloom in the spring."

My grandma was a retired high school social studies teacher. That's probably why she asked crazy questions like "what color is freedom?" Grandma was always trying to make me think.

"Jasmine, finish eating those cupcakes!"

"I'm really not hungry," I said.

I walked over to Grandma and gave her a hug. She started talking about what kind of cake she was going to make when my daddy came home. Last time she made her famous chocolate cake with chocolate icing. This year she said she was going to make a pineapple upside down cake.

"I just wish ..." I kept my mouth shut. I ran out of the kitchen and put on my coat to go home. I didn't want to say what I was thinking, that I just wanted a regular dad, and I just wanted us to be a regular family like we used to be.

CHAPTER 7

Day Four: At Jasmine's Home

It was breakfast time. My mother wanted to know what I wanted to eat. I told her grits and eggs. She said I'd better get ready for school because our whole family planned on attending my graduation in June. June was approaching quickly. I was hoping that my dad would be home in time for my graduation.

I still believed that the only person who really knew the real Jasmine was my dad. He was an electrician before he left for the army. He was the person who always fixed anything that broke in our apartment. Since I was the only child, Dad would take me shopping with him for food and the housecleaning items. I got to pick out some of my favorite foods. Of course my favorite foods were chocolate cupcakes and chocolate milk. Dad would always fill the shopping cart way up to the top. He knew that the food would go fast, so he always bought enough to last us for at least a whole week. When Dad brought the food home, we were all so happy. My mother would make cakes and cookies, and she baked big chickens. The real treats were always made on the weekend when Mom would make chocolate ice cream. When Dad was home, I was always happy and always respectful.

"Jasmine, hurry up!"

"Jasmine, hurry up!" my mother said. She walked by my bedroom and stuck her head in the doorway. She looked at me and said, "Jasmine, I want to prepare your breakfast. Please, please hurry up!"

I crawled out from under my bedspread and walked into the kitchen.

"Now do you really want eggs and grits, Jasmine?" asked my mom.

"I don't eat much," I said.

"Jasmine, please just tell me what you want for breakfast," my mom said sternly.

"Okay, sorry, Mother. I just want toast, eggs, and a very small glass of orange juice," I said. "Mom, I remember every morning we used to eat breakfast in the kitchen with Dad and Grandma. It was nice to be part of a big family. When we ate breakfast, we would always talk about our goals for the day."

"Jasmine, when I was your age, I did not graduate from middle school or high school."

I laughed. "But you did go to adult evening school many years later, and that's how you became a secretary for a law firm."

"That I did. You are so right, Jasmine."

"Mom, Dad better be here next month," I said.

She kissed me on my forehead and gave me the tightest hug. For the first time in my life, I cried because I was so happy. Mom pretended not to notice the smile on my face or the tears. I think it shocked her. Then Mom handed me some tissues to wipe my tears. She wiped hers too. I put my coat on and headed to school. *I better get real serious about this schoolwork*, I said to myself. *I want my mom and dad to be proud of me. And most of all, I want to be proud of myself.*

CHAPTER 8
In DC Woodson's Library Media Center

"Good morning, scholars!" said Mrs. Truth. "Today we will create multimedia presentations in our state-of-the-art library media center."

"Today is the greatest day of a scholar's life," Garvey said. "DC Woodson's scholars won the Eighth Grade Smithsonian Institution Award. The Smithsonian Institution annually gives this award to the eighth grade class that exhibits the most knowledge and enthusiasm in regard to African history and culture."

"Yes!" said the students.

"Yes, scholars," said Garvey. "Who would have believed that in less than a week you could absorb so much information on African history and culture? You have also involved yourselves in so many activities where you have demonstrated your understanding of the information you learned."

"Thanks so much, Master Garvey," Mrs. Truth said.

"You are welcome, Mrs. Truth," he replied. "Now scholars, the Smithsonian Institution award provided us with the funds to create media projects on African history and culture."

"Master Garvey," I murmured.

"Yes, Jasmine," he said.

"I just want to publicly thank you and Mrs. Truth for this wonderful week."

"Why, thank you, Jasmine," Garvey said.

"Okay, scholars, let's get to work," Mrs. Truth said. "Please sit with your assigned team members. Your assignment is to gather information on a specific topic of your choice regarding African history and culture, read and research the information, and then present it in a multimedia format. Take your time and read on your topic of interest very carefully."

I started doing my research on Queen Nefertari (Ne-for-tah-ree) (1292–1225 BC) of the eighteenth dynasty of Egypt. Nefertari was one of the great black queens of Egypt. Queen Nefertari was very active in national affairs, as a participant and leader. Her son was Amenhotep, and her husband was Ramses II, whom today we call Ramses the Great. The schoolwork was easy for me, as I liked to read. My mom and dad were going to be surprised when they got my final report card. They would see that I was really extremely smart.

"Being able to make a video or PowerPoint media presentation is really amazing," said Mrs. Truth. "The success of your presentation is up to each of you. The best team presentation will receive a special award at DC Woodson Middle School's awards assembly on June twenty-fourth."

Everyone in the class started whispering. We did not know that an award was going to be given.

"Scholars, please stop the whispering," Mrs. Truth said. "I know you are very excited about the chance of winning a special award. It will offer you many opportunities to continue studying African history and culture at the same school that our master historian, Garvey, attends. How wonderful is that? It is a great school, a place where you will get a chance to meet some of the world's greatest historians. So please calm down and continue working on your presentations."

I enjoyed working with my group on our multimedia production. I made sure everything got done. I was in charge of the group. It just happened that way because I was so terrific at being a group leader. I was not fooling around, and I was so proud of myself. I'd come a long way from the Jasmine who did not care about attending school or doing her classwork. I was not writing on my desk or telling myself that I was bored. I had learned so much about other aspects of African history. Mrs. Truth was a remarkable teacher. The idea of bringing in Garvey was awesome. He really was knowledgeable about African history and culture. And that trip to the Smithsonian Institute, woo-hoo!

"Jasmine, let's review what we have created," said Lydia.

"Lydia, sometimes you can be a little bit of a show-off! But one thing I do like about you is that you have style. You wear the nicest outfits in the whole class. And—"

"Oh, please, Jasmine, not now!" said Lydia.

"Maybe we should add some background music to the PowerPoint section of our presentation," suggested Omo.

"Good idea!" Lydia said.

"Yes, it's a great idea," I said. "I'm so glad that we worked together on this multimedia project. I believe that the effort we put into this project will surely make us the winners of the special award. I am quite confident that we will be selected. Woo-hoo!"

"May I have every scholar's attention?" said Mrs. Truth. "I believe each group is ready to share its multimedia presentation. Keep in mind that each project will be graded on the basis of the fact that each member of the group participated equally in the creation of the presentation and you provide evidence to prove that. Which group wants to go first?"

Rahim's team members raised their hands first. Rahim's team was so smart. They were even friends after school hours.

Rahim's multimedia presentation was on Makeda's (Queen of Sheba) gifts to King Solomon.

"Wow, what an awesome presentation," I said.

"Jasmine, please don't call out," Mrs. Truth said sternly.

"Sorry, Mrs. Truth!"

"Okay," said Mrs. Truth. "Jasmine and her team will now present their multimedia production."

"The Love Affair that Brought Peace"
Created and produced by Jasmine, Omo, Lydia, and Zahir.
"The Love Affair that Brought about Peace" is our first full-length music and theater work.

Nefertari (1292–1225 BC) was the queen of Kemit (Land of the Blacks). She was heralded the queen who wed for peace. Nefertari was one of the many great Nubian queens. Her marriage to King Ramses II of Egypt is one of the greatest marriages in history. The marriage brought the Hundred Years' War between Nubia and Egypt to an end.

Queen Nefertari

King Ramses II and Queen Nefertari

Everyone seemed to really enjoy our multimedia presentation.

"Jasmine, your team did an excellent job," said Garvey. "Matter of fact, all of you scholars did a superb job."

I thought about what Mrs. Truth said five days ago: "Jasmine, this is a big deal!" I did not believe it actually was …but now I knew I been changed. I also thought about Garvey saying to all the scholars, "Join me on a wonderful journey of learning some aspects of our African history and culture."

CHAPTER 9
Jasmine's Journey

All of DC Woodson Middle School was talking about my team's presentation. I didn't know about Omo, Zahir, or Lydia, but I didn't sleep the entire week before the awards ceremony. Everywhere I went I would hear constant chattering about the fact that my team was sure to be the winner for the African history media presentation. Scholars from other classes came up to me and said how much they enjoyed watching "The Love Affair that Brought Peace." Everyone said they got a chance to see the multimedia presentation during Lunch and Learn.

When the day finally arrived, I was so happy. I never felt so sure about winning, and I never felt so sure about the fact that something so good was going to happen for my team and me. After morning attendance, all the eighth grade scholars jammed into the DC Woodson Middle School auditorium.

Principal Watkins congratulated all the scholars for their participation in making the multimedia projects. As I listened to Mr. Watkins, I became extremely nervous. Finally, the moment that I had been waiting for:

"The winning team for this year's award goes to Rahim's team from Mrs. Truth's class. Their project focused on the Queen of Sheba and the gifts she bestowed on King Solomon. Rahim, will you and your team please come to the front of the auditorium and up to the stage to receive your awards?" said Mr. Watkins.

"We did not win; we did not win!" I said angrily. I ran up the left aisle and was almost out of the auditorium.

"Jasmine, Jasmine, please don't leave!" said Mrs. Truth.

I turned back, looked at Mrs. Truth, and said, "No more auction blocks for me." And to think I spent so much time and energy on this multimedia project. *Well,* I thought, *that's enough for me.*

Suddenly, I stood still for a moment and put my hand on my cheek. Then I started running down the left aisle of the auditorium toward the stage. Everyone started clapping and shouting, "Go Jasmine, go Jasmine." When I got close to the stage, the entire audience stood on their feet and cheered me for what must have been more than two whole minutes. I did something I had never done before. I smiled and actually took a bow. I walked over to Principal Watkins and asked him if I could say a few words, and to my surprise, he handed the microphone to me. My hands were shaking, and I was now crying.

"First of all, I would like to offer an apology to all of you for my negative behavior during this ceremony. Second, I congratulate you, Rahim, and all your team members. Finally, I congratulate all the scholars because, as we know, we are all winners. As Garvey taught us, we must remember that we are the sons and daughters of kings and queens, and we are a great people." Then I said, "Oh, there's one more person who I believe deserves a special thanks, and that is none other than Mrs. Truth."

Mrs. Truth stood up and walked down the left aisle onto the stage. "Jasmine, thanks so much! Also, scholars, please remember that graduation is tomorrow at ten a.m. Please be on time."

CHAPTER 10
Graduation Day

Today was graduation day at DC Woodson's Middle School! I got up at the crack of dawn to see if my dad had made it home in time for my graduation. But Dad was nowhere to be found.

Sadness! I was sure my dad would find his way home for my graduation.

"Jasmine, please don't get upset," my mother moaned, rubbing her forehead in disbelief. "I'm sure your daddy is coming home."

"I sure hope so," I said. "I really expected to see him today. I've waited so long for my daddy."

"It's really very early," my mother said. "Your dad will probably be here in about two hours."

"And if he isn't here, then what?"

My mother didn't answer me.

Two hours later, Mom told me to hurry and get dressed because we were running late. At ten o'clock, Grandma came to pick us up. (Dad had not arrived.) Grandma drove a 2013

Mercedes. She loved to drive that car, especially on special family occasions.

When we arrived at DC Woodson Middle School, it was extremely crowded. I guessed the parents and guests heard that if you arrived late you might not get a seat. I hugged Grandma and my mother and ran off to get in the graduation procession line.

When the graduation started, it was clear to me that my dad was not in attendance. But suddenly, to my surprise, there he was. He hadn't missed my graduation after all. *Happiness!*

"Jasmine," he shouted, "there aren't any seats left so your principal has allowed me to sit up in the front."

"Oh, that's great, Dad!" I shouted back.

After the graduation ceremony, Mrs. Truth came over and I introduced her to my dad. She told him that I had made significant academic improvement in all my subject areas.

"Hey, Jasmine," my dad said as he looked at me, "I'm so proud of you. And I'm sure your mother and grandma are proud too."

"Oh, Dad, I'm so glad you made it home and to my graduation. It's so great to see you!"

"My dear Jasmine, it's great to see you!" he said.

My dad invited Mrs. Truth, Principal Watkins, Lydia, Zahir, and Omo back to our home. Grandma had to make two trips to get everybody in the car. We were a pretty big family now. I talked about my school year the entire ride home. I told my dad about Garvey, the historian. I talked as I ate the wonderful catered lunch my parents had ordered for our guests and me. I even talked about my school year during dinnertime.

Later that evening, after dinner, I asked my dad if he thought it was a good idea for me to attend a summer prep academy at the Smithsonian Institute. I felt my heart thump; I was actually looking forward to high school in September. Especially, since now I was not only acting like a normal thirteen-year-old girl, but I was even speaking like one too. No more yelling, screaming, or hitting anyone.

Dad asked me if the summer academy was a place for kids who needed special help.

"Dad," I said, "the academy is for students who need to sharpen their math, reading, and writing skills."

"In that case, Jasmine, I think it's a great idea for you to attend."

I asked my dad where he had been. He said that he was in the United States Army Reserve Troop 249. Dad also told me he had been stationed in the country of Ghana, located in Africa. He'd had several electrical repair jobs to do at several hospitals in Ghana.

After Dad shared where he had been, I started to realize that one of the most important things a person can do is help someone. And, although I missed my dad every time he left home, I had to remember and respect the fact that he was helping people in Africa.

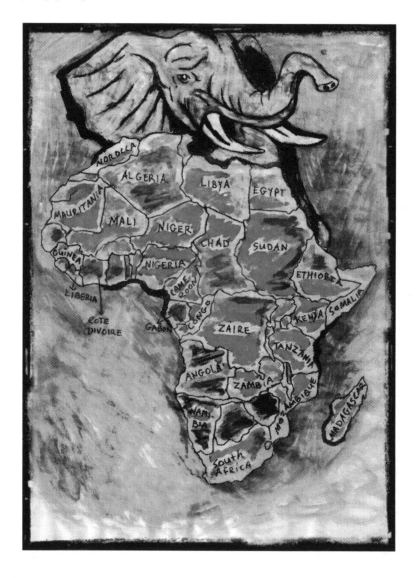

CHAPTER 11
Jasmine's Journey (Summertime)

In the summer of 2014, I attended the Smithsonian Summer Prep Academy in Washington, DC.

The academy seemed worthwhile to me for a couple of reasons. Mrs. Truth, my last homeroom teacher at DC Woodson Middle School, told me that she attended the academy when she was a teenager. And Mrs. Truth had a great influence on my life this past school year. Additionally, the prep academy is known for its reputation in preparing eighth grade graduates for the academic challenges they would encounter in high school.

The majority of my classmates attending the academy were from the DC Woodson Middle School. They appeared to be more knowledgeable than I was and more prepared in all the academic subjects (especially in reading, comprehension, and mathematics). I discovered that I needed to study more. I also discovered the great Smithsonian Institution Libraries.

The libraries became my second home. My favorite librarian was a middle-aged African American woman with beautiful, long black hair and a wonderful smile. Her name was Mrs. Mary. Mrs. Mary took a special interest in me. She assisted me in discovering the hundreds, I mean, thousands of books and magazines in the library. She also showed me how to download information from the Internet. I started reading as much as I possibly could. I spent hours each week in the library.

I like it here. It's interesting here. I need to be here. I want to be here. I like it here, I wrote in my journal. *Some folks think that troublemakers always remain troublemakers. And you know what? That's not true. I am not a troublemaker. I like it here. I like it here.*

Then I took out my book on African history and culture.

Next I took out my sketchbook and started drawing pictures of me completing my summer prep academy assignments. *Hmmm,* I thought, *I'll draw a picture of me asking the librarian for help with one of my research assignments. And I'll draw a picture of my family and me attending my future high school graduation.*

I'd really been thinking a lot. I could sit here and continue to draw pictures and write in my journal. Everyone in my summer prep academy had a hobby. Some of my classmates played baseball or basketball. Some played an instrument, such as piano or guitar. I, however, preferred writing and drawing. *Hmmm …I'll ask Dad if he can afford to send me to an art school for some private art lessons. I love to draw.*

The only one who really knew me, and how I felt about almost everything, was my awesome dad. I was glad he was home. Last night, I had overheard him in the kitchen telling my mother that he was not going away anymore. That was great news. I started thinking about the fact that I came from a great people. *I must be great too!*

***

JASMINE'S FAVORITE HISTORICAL FIGURES

Dr. John Henrik Clarke

Dr. John Henrik Clarke was a professor of African history. Professor Clarke's writings and works are known throughout the world. He wanted all African Americans to be knowledgeable about their history. Dr. Clarke's favorite saying was "You must know where you came from to know who you are and what you must do."

Queen Mother Moore

Queen Mother Moore was a self-educated elder who worked very hard in the struggle for African people. Queen Mother would always wear beautiful African clothes to show that she was clearly proud of her African identity. She was known for her courage in fighting for equal rights for African Americans. She was known for her teaching, speaking, and action. The question Queen Mother Moore would always bring to her people was "Don't you know that you are Africans?" Queen

Mother Moore would explain that even though you were not born in Africa, you were still an African.

President Kwame Nkrumah

Kwame Nkrumah (Kwa-may N-Kroo-mah) was president of Ghana in West Africa from 1960 to 1966. Kwame Nkrumah was given the title "Osagyefo" (O-sah-ge-fo), which meant hero and warrior. Kwame's platform was based on African unity and freedom from colonialism.

Nina Simone

Nina Simone was an African American singer, songwriter, pianist, and civil rights activist, widely associated with jazz music. Nina Simone worked in a broad range of styles, including classical, jazz, blues, folk, rhythm and blues, and gospel. She always stated that there was no excuse for African American children not knowing the history of Africa.

Marian Anderson

Marian Anderson was born in Philadelphia in 1902. She always dreamed of becoming a singer. At an early age, Marian was denied entrance to music school because she was an African American. She did not like the fact that racism existed in the United States and refused to give up hope of becoming a singer. She started to perform for small segregated audiences. All the audiences that heard Marian enjoyed her singing. She eventually became the first African American to sing at the Metropolitan Opera House in New York City. Although it was not Marian Anderson's goal, she changed American history and proved the right of people everywhere to follow their dreams.

Malcolm X

Malcolm X was born in 1925. He fought for equal rights for African Americans. He also saw the struggle that black people went through as a global struggle. Malcolm X was assassinated because he was a person who fought for the liberation of black people.

Marcus Garvey

Marcus Garvey was born in Saint Ann's Bay, Jamaica, West Indies. Marcus was the creator of one of the largest groups of black people. In the 1920s, he organized the Universal Negro Improvement Association. He felt that black people as a race were always engaged in a struggle for survival. Marcus Garvey taught black people that they should be self-reliant and have pride in their African heritage.

Hatshepsut

Hatshepsut was the first woman in Egyptian history to become a pharaoh. Hatshepsut was also the first warrior queen in African history. Her temple still stands in the Valley of the Kings in Egypt.

Neta-Kerti

Queen Neta-Kerti, known as the most beautiful woman of her time, was a ruler for twelve years. She was in charge of giving directions for the completion of the third pyramid of Men-Ka-Ra at Giza.

Imhotep, the Father of Medicine

Imhotep was often referred to as the God of Medicine. He was a physician who diagnosed over two hundred diseases. Imhotep was also the builder of the Step Pyramid.

GLOSSARY

accomplishment: 1. An activity that you can do well. 2. Something that has been achieved successfully.

activist: A person who campaigns for political or social change.

Africa: The world's second-largest most populous continent.

African: A person from Africa. Africans are natives or inhabitants of Africa and people of African descent.

African American: 1. A black American. 2. A citizen of the United States who has total or partial ancestry from Africa.

ago/amee: "May I have your attention?" and "You may have my attention," respectively.

ancestor: Person from whom you are descended.

ancient: Belonging to the very distant past.

ancient Egypt: An ancient civilization in northeastern Africa, concentrated on the lower reaches of the Nile River in what is now the country of Egypt.

annually: Once a year, every year.

archaeology: The study of ancient history through the examination of objects, structures, and old materials dug up from old sites.

artifact: An object made by a human being, typically an item of cultural or historical interest.

auction block: Or block, a platform from which an auctioneer sells; the old courthouse where slaves were sold from the auction block, sold to the highest bidder.

bid: To offer a price for something.

bookmark: A strip of leather, cardboard, fabric, or material used to mark a place in a book.

boring: Dull and uninteresting.

caring: A feeling of concern or interest.

civilization: 1. An advanced stage of human development in which people in a society behave well toward each other and share a common culture. 2. The society, culture, and way of life of a particular area or period.

culture: The arts, customs, and institutions of a nation, people, or group.

descendant: A person who is descended from a particular ancestor.

diaspora: The dispersion of any people from their original homeland.

fragment: A small part that has broken off or come from something larger.

freedom: 1. The state of not being a prisoner or slave. 2. Not being affected by something undesirable.

great: 1. Considerably above average in extent, amount, or strength. 2. Considerably above average in quality.

hate: Feel very strong dislike for.

hero: A person who is admired for his courage or outstanding achievements.

heroine: A woman admired for her courage or outstanding achievements.

historian: An expert in history.

history: The study of past events.

hostage: A person held prisoner in an attempt to make other people give in to a demand.

intact: Not damaged or impaired in any way; complete.

intelligent: Good at learning, understanding, and thinking.

king: Male ruler of an independent state.

King Solomon: The wisest man who ever lived.

Martin Luther King Jr.: African American pastor, activist, humanitarian, and leader in the African American civil rights movement.

mighty: Very strong or powerful.

murmur: Say something quietly.

mystery: Something that is difficult or impossible to understand or explain.

palace: A grand residence, especially a royal residence or the home of a head of state or some other high-ranking dignitary, such as a king or queen.

pharaoh: A ruler in ancient Egypt.

portrait: A painting, drawing, or photograph of a particular person.

public intellectual: A well-known, learned person whose written works and other social and cultural contributions are recognized not only by academic audiences and readers, but also by members of society in general.

pyramid: A very large stone structure with a square or triangle base and sloping sides that meet in a point at the top.

queen: Female ruler of an independent state.

Queen of Sheba: A seeker of truth and wisdom; she traveled on a camel to Jerusalem to meet King Solomon of Israel and test his knowledge with lots of questions and riddles. When she visited King Solomon, she brought frankincense, myrrh, gold, and precious jewels.

research: The study of materials and sources in order to establish facts and find new conclusions.

scholar: A person studying at an advanced level.

Sierra Leone: A country in West Africa bordered by Guinea to the northeast, Liberia to the southeast, and the Atlantic Ocean to the southwest.

Smithsonian Institution: A group of museums and research centers in Washington, DC, administered by the US government. The Smithsonian was established in 1846 to increase the "diffusion of knowledge."

synthesize: Combine parts into a connected whole.

tomb: 1. A burial place consisting of a stone structure built above ground, or an underground vault. 2. A monument to a dead person built over his or her burial place.

video: 1. A system of recording and reproducing moving images using magnetic tape. 2. A movie or other recording on magnetic tape or in digital form.

BIBLIOGRAPHY

Adams, Barbara Eleanor. *John Henrik Clarke: Master Teacher.* Brooklyn, NY: A & B Publishers Group, 2000.

Conversations on African history and culture with Queen Mother Nina, Takada Walls, and Maud Holloway (deceased).

Jackson, Barbara Dean. *We Are the Children of the Great Ancient Africans.* Brooklyn, NY: Black News, 1981.

Jimbaumprocinwarn. *William Negotiating for Gara,* video. You Tube: https://www.youtube.com/watch?v=3S2LAyFg4zk, uploaded March 30, 2008.

Lewin, Arthur. *Africa Is Not a Country: It's a Continent.* Milltown, NJ: Claredon Publishing Company, 1990.

MissMusu21. *Exploring a Day in the Life of Sierra Leone,*
a short documentary film. http://www.bing.com/videos/
search?q=exploring+a+day+in+the+life+of+sierra+leone&
FORM=VIRE2#view=detail&mid=9AB08836BDE0DD3
6D6E69AB08836BDE0DD36D6E6, uploaded April 5, 2011.

Smithsonian Institution website, http://www.si.edu.

ABOUT THE ILLUSTRATOR

Link Lacaille grew up in Brooklyn, New York. Link is skilled in graphic arts, drawing, and oil painting. His artworks have been featured in his original children's books as well as in several of his family's and friends' homes.

Printed in the United States
By Bookmasters